KERB
STAIN
BOYS

KERB STAIN BOYS

ALEX WHEATLE

Barrington Stoke

*To those who were told they'd
never amount to much*

First published in 2018 in Great Britain by
Barrington Stoke Ltd
18 Walker Street, Edinburgh, EH3 7LP

www.barringtonstoke.co.uk

Text © 2018 Alex Wheatle

A CIP catalogue record for this book is available
from the British Library upon request

ISBN: 978-1-78112-809-1

Printed in China by Leo

CONTENTS

CHAPTER ONE

Detention

It was almost home time. Sixty seconds to go before we went missing for the weekend. Then, *boof*. A bottle of water slapped the back of my head.

I spun around. I felt water dripping down my back. I heard mad giggles. I could feel the heat of Caldonia Lake's eyes burning gas-rings into me. Her tongue was ripe for a cuss attack.

"Don't you *ever* make jokes about my eyebrows, Capleton!" Caldonia spat.

So I had just branded her the blue forehead smurf queen, but she had called me a skinny runner bean first.

I shot out of my chair and hyper-footed over to her.

She stood up. "What?" she challenged. Her gob spray polluted my cheeks. "You wanna fist-off now? Some man you are, wanting to war with a girl."

"I'll quit yabbering on about your brows if you stop going on about my height."

Terror shot out of his seat as if it had an eject button. He rushed up to me, chin in the air. "Lay one thumb on my queen and your lips are gonna be separated," Terror warned.

I body-barged Terror out of my way. "Get out of my space!" I said to him. "This has got shit all to do with you."

"*Fight, fight, fight*," the classroom chanted.

"Stop!" Mr Wyatt intervened. He snapped a textbook shut and marched towards us. "Caldonia, Terry and Capleton, you're staying. The rest of you can go."

Table legs and chairs screeched and scraped. The buzzer sounded. My year ten Maths class barged out of the classroom. Terror, his green eyes sizzling, looked at me like he wanted the bell to clang to start round two. I wasn't sure if I was up to it. He was shorter than me but ripped and crusty. His fists weren't small. Caldonia sat back down and took out a small make-up mirror from her rucksack. She checked her eyebrows – tattooed blue. They dipped and curled like micro roller-coasters.

"I'm warning you, Briggy," Terror said as he pointed a finger at me. "*Don't* trouble my queen."

"I'm not your freaking queen," Caldonia cut in. "And I don't need you to do my warring for me. I can look after myself."

"Stop," Wyatt barked.

"But ..." Terror began, and tailed off. He returned to his seat.

3

"What's a matter with you three?" asked Wyatt. "I thought you were friends?"

Terror and me had been bredrens since we were both wrapped in nappies. But ever since Terror had locked on his lust for Caldonia Lake, issues had short-circuited between us.

Wyatt glared at me. "Capleton, can you apologise to Caldonia? And Caldonia, say sorry to Capleton."

I looked away. *Why should I be the one to apologise first? Caldonia started this shit. I just wanna get out of her cussing range.*

"OK," I said, facing up to her. "Sorry for branding you the blue forehead smurf queen."

Caldonia grinned an *I got the better of you* grin.

"Caldonia?" said Wyatt. "Apologise."

Caldonia gave me an evil eye-pass, scoping me from my baby toe to eyebrow corner. She then kissed her teeth for ten seconds and shook her head. Finally, she said, "Sorry." I could barely hear her. "Sorry for calling you a long skinny runner bean with a crusty bread forehead."

Did she have to repeat the full cuss?

Wyatt scoped Terror hard. "Terry," Wyatt said. "You owe me an apology too."

Terror stared at the floor. "Sorry."

Wyatt returned to his seat. "You all still have detention," he said. He tip-tapped his fingers on his desk. There was an uneasy silence. Terror broke it.

"Why it's only us three doing time?" Terror asked. "Early B and Flabba Holt were raging at each other."

"A bottle was thrown," said Mr Wyatt. "You have to have boundaries."

"I didn't fling any bottle," I said.

Wyatt looked at me like I ate his logarithm charts. To avoid his spotlight, I looked out the window. Two teachers in Day-glo yellow were on patrol at the school gates. A male fed stood on the other side of the road – there had been a shanking outside school a few weeks ago. The kids of South Crongton High streamed out. A 250 bus pulled up and there was a mad rush to get on it.

I sensed Terror's temper brewing behind me. I glanced past him. Caldonia sat cross-legged, examining her nails. I couldn't lie. She was the coolest chick in our year. And the prettiest. Long black curls topped her off neatly. Thick mascara glammed up her eyes. Chocolate-brown lipstick sexed up her lips. Even year eleven bruvs peeked a second glance at her curves. Chicks wanted to look like her and Terror wanted to star on *Love Island* with her.

"I'll be back in a minute," said Wyatt. "I suggest that if you have any homework – start it."

Terror kissed his teeth and turned his back. Caldonia didn't look up from her nails.

Wyatt scoped us hard again. "At least take out a book and read."

I considered grabbing the book I'm reading – *Noughts & Crosses* – from my rucksack but thought better of it. Didn't want Terror and Caldonia to think I was a slave to the page.

"Stay here!" Wyatt warned. "If any of you so much as put a toe outside this classroom, then you can say hello to detentions for the next week."

He closed the door behind him.

Terror stood up. "You know what?" he said. "Bomb this! Mum gave me two ten notes to put on the gas and electric on the way home. We only had a few pence on it when I left this morning. She's gonna cuss me hard if I land back at my ends late and the electric has run out."

Caldonia looked up and said, "Then wheel back to your slab right now. What's stopping you?"

"He's on his last warning," I said. "If he goes all ghost on his detention again, he's getting—"

"*He* can speak for himself." Terror cut my flow. "You wanna lock-down your tongue, Briggy, or it's gonna find your long ass in tribulation one day."

"You know what?" I told Terror. "Just bring it any time!"

Terror crackled back into his seat, but he didn't respond.

I didn't love being tall. There was almost six foot of my long runner-bean ass. When shit happened behind teachers' backs, they'd turn around and point their fingers at me. Even when I wasn't being aggressive, some peeps thought I was. I didn't really wanna maul Terror, my best bredren.

Caldonia studied her nails again. "They can give me detention till dawn o'clock," she said. "I don't give a flying squiddly."

"Don't you wanna step home?" I asked.

"Nothing to step home for," she said. "Apart from Mum sploshing dinner on my plate that's been in the fridge for four days. Dad's still on unemployment island. Can't watch zero squat on TV cos we haven't got a dish and the nearest I'm gonna get to a tablet is if I jack some brain-ache pills from Dagthorn's shop."

I glanced at Caldonia's raggedy trousers and nibbled shoes.

"You can watch shit on your phone," I suggested.

Caldonia zipped open her bag and took out a mobile phone that was as thick as the Bible.

9

"I hear you," I said.

"I don't love school and I don't love home," Caldonia said. "The only joy I get is when I glam up my face with a liccle make-up to make me feel on point in the morning. But, oh no! *You* have to stomp all over that, don't you, Capleton?"

"What d'you expect if you're branding me the *skinny shard to rule 'em all*," I said to defend myself. "I'm not gonna let that pass."

Caldonia kissed her teeth for even longer than ten seconds. Her eyes narrowed like she was thinking of a most devious plan. She took a half-smoked rocket from her purse and straightened it out. She fired it up with a lighter, sucked on it hard, then blew perfect smoke rings towards the ceiling. I didn't love her ways but she was as cool as a penguin sliding on one foot down an iceberg.

"So you're not satisfied with getting us

detention," I said. "You wanna get us expelled too."

Caldonia side-eyed me. "Capleton, lock-tight your lips, man, and leave me alone."

"Can I have a sample?" asked Terror.

"Don't flood the butt," she said. She passed the rocket on to Terror. Weed smoke filled the room. The sweet smell tunnelled up my nostrils. My gaze locked on to the classroom door. *Oh my days. If Wyatt comes back now, we'll be terminated. My mum will go psycho on me. It won't be pretty.*

Terror had taken three pulls from the rocket. He scoped Caldonia like he wanted to make babies. "So what d'you say, Caldonia?" Terror said. "Can I slide over to your slab later on?"

Caldonia snatched the rocket from Terror's grasp. She took one last drag before she killed it. "What did I tell you?" she raised her voice. "My paps don't like me bringing any kerb stains to our gates."

"I'm not a kerb stain," Terror protested.

"*Yes*, you are," Caldonia argued. "You live in the south ends of the estate, so you're one hundred per cent, original, grimy, stainy side of the kerb."

"That's cold," Terror said.

I covered my mouth to block my giggles. Terror side-eyed me and spotted my laughing eyes. Then he switched his attention back to Caldonia. He was still as high as a hot-air balloon. "So, as you're my queen now," Terror said, "what d'you say we go out – grooving over the ice rink or licking down some skittles or something?"

Caldonia bored her eyes into Terror like she wanted to toast him with a hot coal. "Listen me good, Terror," she said. "I'm not gonna press the replay on this one. You have a bit of cuteness going on and your muscles are hard in all the right places. You're a bit dense in the brain section but you can get away with that cos you have a liccle funny side that I like. But I'm *not* your freaking queen. Nobody owns me. *Nobody!* Not even my dad."

"But ..." Terror replied. "But we meshed tongues the other day—"

"Yeah! And?" Caldonia fired back. "Just cos we tickled tonsils it doesn't mean you've got a receipt to claim my ass. Do I have an Amazon label on my butt?"

I studied Caldonia's bumper – I gave it eleven outta ten.

"So what did it mean?" Terror wanted to know.

"It meant that in that moment I wanted to bend tongues with you," Caldonia said. She leaned forward to press home her point.

I was feeling it for Terror. His ego was getting smashed.

Caldonia wasn't finished. "It doesn't mean I wanna glam up in all white and make promises to a preacher. Are you comprehending me?"

Terror nodded. What else could he do? There was an awkward silence for the next two minutes. I think we all wanted Wyatt to return but no one would admit it. I decided to rest my gaze on the clock fixed to the classroom wall.

"Being someone's partner is not on my agenda," Terror said to Caldonia. "I'm only fifteen for fruck's sake. Even when I reach the mad old age of *thirty*, I'm not on that programme. But I was just thinking that we could flex – you know, kinda friends with benefits. Maybe after that, switch it to a long-term thing."

Caldonia stood up and bit her top lip. I waited for the cuss attack. She hot-stepped over to

Terror like she was an assassin with a deadline. He leaned back as she fired up her tongue.

"Listen me proper," Caldonia said. "Maybe me and you can have laughs and jokes and make out when I feel like it, but you and me will *never* be a long-term thing. Are you comprehending?"

"Why not?" Terror wanted to know.

"*Why not?*" Caldonia repeated. "I'm gonna clarify this situation, so don't get offended."

Man. I didn't love the sound of that. I was glad I wasn't in Terror's socks.

Caldonia went on, "For your information, you haven't got shit-all going for you. Your Maths is even sadder than mine. The refugees in this school write better English than you and there are seven-year-old kids in the Congo who are handier with a laptop. You know I'm not wrong."

Ouch! It was hard to watch. This wasn't a car smash, it was a train wreck.

Caldonia placed her hands on Terror's desk. She leaned in even closer to him. Her nose was an inch away from his. It wasn't jokes any more. A referee woulda blown mighty hard on a whistle to stop it.

"So in a few years' time, what can you offer me?" she said. "You'll probably end up working in a 99p store wearing some sad apron with a cheapo hat to match."

Terror tried to bluster away his shame. His lips moved but nothing came out for five seconds. "I've got plans," he said at last. "Serious plans."

Caldonia smiled like she was thinking up something devious. She then stood up and glanced at me. I didn't wanna get my ego beaten too, so I stared at the floor.

"And the same goes for you, Capleton," Caldonia said. "What are you good at?"

I thought about it. My Drama was on point. My History wasn't too tragic. I didn't wanna think about my English or Maths. I only used IT for Facebook, Instagram and Twitter. "I was in the table tennis team last year," I managed. "We got to the semi-finals."

Caldonia stepped towards me. She shook her head like I was a cute Labrador that had to be put down. "The school hasn't had a table tennis team since Mr Madeley left," she said. "We haven't even got a netball team for our year after Lisa Dempsey started that brawl with the Joan Benson Academy chicks. That fight was the last straw."

"But ..." Terror said.

"But what?" Caldonia said, and wheeled around to confront Terror again. "I'm gonna give you a dose of realness. Apart from busting jokes in class, you two aren't shit-hot at anything. Not that I can see anyhow. Squiddly-squat. Nothing."

That stung like a mega-size wasp. Terror dropped his head. I didn't know where to look.

Another awkward silence. Caldonia parked her curvy self down and examined her nails some more. What could we say? She was in a higher group than us in almost everything. I'd heard her speak French and Spanish. She could be even more top ranking if she bothered to do the work. I willed for Wyatt to come back.

"We've got plans," Terror said, after a while.

"What plans?" Caldonia wanted to know.

Terror glanced at me. He didn't tell me about any plans. *What's he on?*

"We're gonna ... we're gonna rob a post office," Terror said. "That's been our mission for weeks. Nuff plans have been made. We're on it."

My heart stopped to have a convo with my ears. It took a long second to pump a beat again. *Did he just spill that?* I thought. *Is he that charged? He only had three puffs.* I opened my mouth but nothing came out.

Meanwhile, Caldonia collapsed into a heap of giggleness. "You two?" she stuttered. "Rob a—? Ha ha ha! Oh my days, this is too much! Too funny. A post office!"

I was offended to the core. It was madness and it wasn't happening, but she didn't have to chuckle her ribs out like that.

I looked at Terror and his eyebrows had hardened. "I'm serious," Terror said. "No jokes!"

Caldonia held her belly to keep her guts in place. "Slap my dragons," she chuckled. "I get some jokes today. You two rob—"

Wyatt returned. He was carrying folders and textbooks and he placed them on his desk. He sniffed at the air but didn't say anything. He didn't look too happy.

"Can we step now?" asked Terror.

Wyatt sat down. I scoped him hard. Wyatt hadn't shaved for a couple of days. His tie was off-key. Stress lines shot off the corners of his eyes. His guts spilled over his belt. He had let himself go since I started in year seven. He meshed his fingers together. "Why can't you three understand?" Wyatt said. "You can't carry on like this. This is a vital time of year for you all. In just a few months you'll be taking your GCSEs."

Caldonia covered her mouth as she kept trying to block her chuckles. The post office mission was probably still giving her jokes.

"Something funny?" Wyatt asked.

"No, sir," Caldonia replied. "I'm not busting chuckles about you. Honest."

Wyatt took in a breath. "You'll be out there in the big wide world before you know it," Wyatt said. "It's time to *grow* up and act like year tens, *not* year sevens."

"Can we step now?" Terror repeated.

Wyatt thought about it. He looked like he wanted to step home too. "Go on, get out of my classroom. I expect better behaviour next lesson."

CHAPTER TWO

The Plan

Caldonia was at the back of the classroom but she made it out first. Terror and I caught up with her in the hall. Her face was still full of giggles. "You're being serious?" Caldonia asked. "You two are gonna jack a post office?"

"Yep," Terror said with a nod. "Most def."

Caldonia turned her eyes to spotlight me. They had question marks in them. I didn't wanna look lame in front of her. "Er, yeah," I said. "We're on it."

"Which one?" she asked.

I wasn't sure if Caldonia was taking us serious.

"The one on Crongton Broadway," Terror replied. "Rich people step there, so it should have more Gs in the tills."

We made it out into the playground. The Day-glo teachers and the fed had gone. I couldn't believe the way the convo was shaping.

"How much d'you reckon you'll jack?" Caldonia wanted to know.

"Um," Terror said. "Maybe about five big ones. Could be ten. Might be more if luck blesses us that day. I'm gonna have to get myself a fat wallet."

"And what are you gonna spend it on?" Caldonia pressed us.

"Um ..." Terror started.

"We're gonna invest it," I cut in. "So we can set up our own business by the time we've booted school to the kerb."

"What business?" Caldonia asked. "You can't

just start any business. You have to know what you're doing, otherwise it'll go all wrong."

We stepped out of the school gates. "We haven't decided yet," I replied.

"No, we haven't," Terror said. "There's nuff options out there."

The sun blazed. We trekked towards Dagthorn's store in the middle of the estate. I was kinda hoping that Caldonia would step her own way now, and that would put a fat full stop to this convo, but she was hungry to learn more. She had never stepped with us outside school before.

"You can't just bounce up to the counter and ask the assistant to fill your bags with Gs," Caldonia said. "You've gotta carry something to show you're not playing."

"We're looking after that," Terror replied. "That's all on the agenda."

We reached Dagthorn's. Hardback road bruvs slobbered over Captain Crunch ice lollies. Younger kids got high on sugar rushes. Year nine and ten chicks scoped the celebrity mags.

Terror went to top up his gas card and electric key. He didn't love doing that when kids were around – no one wanted to be branded a ghetto meter kid. Caldonia and I waited outside. We watched a crew of kerb rats doing wheelies on their bikes.

Caldonia looked at me hard while Terror was at the counter. "Capleton," she said. "Are you two *really* on this?"

I thought about it. I remembered her words. *I'm gonna give you a dose of realness*, she'd said. *You two aren't shit-hot at anything.* That hurt like a body-slam from the Hulk.

"We're on this for real," I replied. "Most def."

Her eyelashes fluttered like crows in a storm.

A year-seven kid burst out of Dagthorn's store clutching a Captain Crunch Super Duper choc lolly. Dagthorn's daughter, Simone, hot-footed after him. This kid scorched along Parchmore Drive, took a sharp left into an alley and was gone. Simone gave up the hunt and cursed the full ghetto dictionary of bad words. The hardback road bruvs laughed.

Caldonia nodded. "You know what?" she said. "Your mission can win the gold. Just keep your eyes below the CCTV radar. It's harder for CCTV to recognise you if you're looking down."

Terror returned and said, "Did you see that? I know him. Tristan Palmer. His fam lives in the slab opposite me – Newton House."

We headed down Mulse Street, where there was a small concrete skate park. Graffiti covered everything. Kids surfed over concrete ramps on skateboards and mountain bikes. Caldonia linked arms with Terror – I'd never seen that before.

She waved her lashes at him and said, "Reel me in on this."

"You what?" Terror asked.

"Rope me in to your mission," Caldonia said. "That post office on Crong Broadway probably has more than ten grand. Maybe fifteen. They've got a foreign-currency counter, so they'll have to be stocked up with dollars and euros. And I can't remember the last time someone jacked a post office in Crongton. The gangs are concentrating on off-licences, barber shops, Alabama chicken sheds and bookies."

"What are you gonna do?" I challenged Caldonia. "Stick up the post office with your make-up mirror? And tell them, *Nobody move, nobody get hurt, I want new shoes and a name-brand shirt*."

I chuckled at my own spitting skills. Caldonia wasn't impressed. Not impressed at all.

"You think I can't do shit?" Caldonia raised her tones. "I'm as hardback as any of you bruvs. What's your issue with me, Briggs?"

I hated peeps calling me Briggs. It sounded too official, like I was the captain of the chess team or something. I much preferred Briggy.

"I haven't got an issue with you," I replied.

"Then why are you forever bashing my buzz?" Caldonia said. "Since I've been linking with Terror, you've been burning about it. Envy's munching your ego."

"I'M NOT JEALOUS!" I yelled.

"Simmer down, you two," Terror cut in.

"Then tell your bredren not to question my kerb credentials," Caldonia spat. "I'm from the ends. I *can* do shit. When I say I'm on a mission, I'm not playing."

She flicked me another hard look.

We stepped on.

"Caldonia," Terror said. "If you wanna be on this mission, then I won't object. Maybe you can be our lookout."

I cut my eyes at Terror.

"Sweet," Caldonia said. She grinned. "If we make ten grand, that'll be three thousand, three hundred and thirty-three each."

Her maths was up to spec.

"With the Gs we make, I'll open a sports bar," Terror said. "But not in Crongton. I'll open it in an ends where peeps don't bitch about paying for their cocktails and munchies."

"Three grand and a bit wouldn't buy you a front door and a bar counter," I said.

"There you go again, Briggs," Caldonia said. She gave me another side-eye. "Always popping peeps' buzzes. If Terror wants to dream of opening a sports bar, then allow him."

Caldonia had hit Terror's sweet spot. He

show-boated his teeth like he'd been invited to Beyoncé's after party. "Thanks for having my spine, Princess," Terror said.

"I'm *not* your pissing princess," Caldonia snapped. "And what's more, this is where I step off."

We had reached the east ends of South Crongton estate. The slabs of Somerleyton, Drockwell and Larkhall loomed over us like huge dominoes.

"Can't I stroll you home?" Terror pleaded.

"Are your ears working?" Caldonia asked.

"Yeah, of course they are," Terror replied.

"Then how comes you don't hear me?" Caldonia said loudly. "My fam *don't* wanna see me stalked to my gates by a kerb stain. They'll give me grief about it."

"I'm not—" Terror began.

"Yes, you *are*!" Caldonia yelled.

"But aren't you a kerb stain too?" I cut in.

Caldonia paused, then replied, "Yeah, we are. But my fam don't see it that way."

Awkward moment number six. Terror dropped his head. I glanced backwards. Suddenly, Caldonia pulled Terror towards her. She ran her hands in his hair, then cupped his cheeks. They pressed lips and bent tongues like they were auditioning for *Fifty Shades of Crongton*. Terror grabbed Caldonia's bumper and squeezed it as if pips might come out of it. I'm not gonna lie, rich green jealousy chomped my long, skinny ass. I wasn't even Terror's best bredren now.

The lip-smackers came up for air. Terror had his *I'm gonna have sex soon* grin on. Caldonia took out her small mirror and fixed her brown lipstick. "That'll keep ya till tomorrow," she said.

"Yeah," Terror said.

"Now, back to the mission," Caldonia said. "We have to check out the post office tomorrow and see how many staff they've got behind the counter. Also, we need an escape route. We gotta scope out the closest exits. We gotta decide what direction we're flying to after."

"We can scorch down Blowhawk Lane," Terror suggested.

"But we've got school tomorrow," I said.

Terror's eyes were still going funny – he had caught a bad love bug.

Caldonia pulled a face at me and mocked, "*But we've got school tomorrow. We're missing* from school tomorrow morning, Briggs. We'll link by Dagthorn's."

"But what about—" I protested.

"What about nothing!" Caldonia said. "If we're doing this, we have to set things up neatly."

"She's on point." Terror nodded.

"Nine o'clock on the bang," Caldonia said. "Don't even think about being late. All right, I'm gone."

We watched her step towards Somerleyton House. I couldn't deny it. She had the sexiest stroll since Beyoncé shook her curves at the Super Bowl. I looked sideways at Terror. The love bug still infected him. He didn't move till Caldonia vanished behind Drockwell House.

CHAPTER THREE

Blueberry Condoms

I punched Terror's arm. Hard. "Are you cadazy?" I yelled at him. "Jack the post office on Crong Broadway? Did someone drop a basketball on your head from a mad height in gym today?"

Terror shook his head. "Caldonia's right about you," he said. "You love bashing peeps' buzzes. Briggy, we can do this. It's not like a bank."

We started to roll back to our ends.

"Does Dagthorn's sell condoms?" Terror said. "Maybe I can get one of them juicy flavours – blueberry? I might jack 'em if Dagthorn's daughter isn't scoping me. She always scopes me when—"

"Can you pull your dick outta your head for a sec?" I said.

"But do I look like a real t'ief?"

"Yes, you do!" I told him.

"Keep your curls on, bruv," Terror said. "I just want safe sex. My mum will be proper proud of me."

I didn't wanna think about Terror bumping thighs with Caldonia. I wanted to reel us back from the crime spree he had planned. "D'you think the judge will care that it's not a freaking bank?" I pointed out. "We'll be slurping porridge and counting cold bricks in cells for the longest time. Haven't you got an uncle who's doing bird?"

"Yeah," Terror replied. "But he never planned his missions. He just went for it if he didn't have anything to eat in the morning."

"If we keep on stepping down this lane, we'll be joining him inside," I said.

Terror flashed a grin. "Briggy, stop being on the down-low, bruv. Close your eyes and goggle-box it. No more shopping for your trainers in TK Maxx. No more fake Barcelona shirts from Crong market. No more getting your cheapo chicken from Alabama chicken sheds. No more older brothers trimming your curls with grimy shavers."

Terror wasn't wrong about the chicken from Alabama chicken sheds. And my curls looked bad. My older bruv, Kingsley, tried his best, but after he finished snipping, my Afro looked like locusts had nibbled it.

"I thought you wanted to invest the Gs?" I reminded Terror.

"Yeah, but we can still treat ourselves," Terror said. "Trust me, Briggy, chicks are gonna be on you when they sniff the Gs. Haven't you seen the hotel scene in *Straight Outta Compton* when NWA are on tour? That's gonna be us, bruv. Caldonia and me, you and your fit chick in a six-star hotel. We'll be sinking the crumbliest and juiciest cheesecakes ordered from the Cheesecake Lounge. And then you'll get to have sex in an emperor-size bed. Dream about the wonderfulness of that."

I couldn't help it. I imagined a chocolate and strawberry cheesecake sliding down my throat. I also imagined Jennifer Caltrao, the uber-fit Portuguese chick in my English class, dipping her chocolate flake in a strawberry mousse beside me. Then reality pricked my brain.

"We'll be recognised," I said. "Peeps will see us going in and out of the post office and they'll know who we are. You're talking about Crongton Broadway. Even the flies carry CCTV on their backs."

Terror thought about it. "We'll be carrying

something to hold 'em up, and we'll jack some of those plain white masks from the art room at school," he said. "We'll put those on before we rush the post office. And we won't be garmed in school uniform. That's a definite no-no."

"Terror," I said. "This is stupidocious. Cadazy—"

"I tell you what's stupidocious," Terror cut me off. "Trying to get a job that pays you sweet when we're done with school. Stupidocious is putting on a tie and going to interview after pissing interview when you know they're not gonna give you shit. Deep down, Briggy, you know that's the truth. Caldonia's not wrong when she says we aren't shit-hot at anything. What can we do?"

I couldn't answer him.

"Teachers like Wyatt don't even try with us any more," Terror went on. "They only take notice when we're bantering and making some noise. They'll be high-fiving if we manage to get a job serving skinny freaking lattes."

I couldn't argue. That was how it was.

"And where's that gonna get us?" Terror kept on. "We'll be living with our parents till we're fifty."

Living with my mum and dad till I'm fifty? The idea of it froze my arteries.

Maybe Terror wasn't so cadazy after all.

CHAPTER FOUR

Han Solo Laser Blasters

We stepped to Terror's slab – Eldridge House. A bruv with grey whiskers in council garms was trying to unblock the rubbish chute. A carpenter was fixing a window frame on the ground floor.

"Fake guns," Terror said.

"What?" I said.

"Fake guns," Terror repeated. "That's how we're gonna rock it. We need fake guns that look like the real blazing deal. Toy ones, you know – for kids. You haven't got anything at your yard, have you?"

I gave Terror a funny look. "My bruv is twenty-two," I reminded him. "I'm fifteen. Why would I have any toy guns in my yard?"

Terror thought about it. "Yeah, Briggy, I hear you on that one."

"Haven't you got liccle cousins?" I said. "Everton and his bruv, whassisname?"

Terror's eyes lit up like a lighthouse at the dark end of the sea. "Neville!" he yelled. "Yes, Everton's eight and Neville's six. Good thinking, Briggy. We'll march to their slab right now."

"Before we step off," I said, "will they really have something we can use? Don't wanna step there for nothing. It's a long trod."

Terror checked his stride. He grinned like Wonder Woman had promised to dirty-dance with him at the school prom. "My mum bought them *Star Wars* laser guns for Christmas last year," Terror said. "We're in the game."

He held up his right palm in the air and I slapped it hard. "Yeah!" I said with a nod. "We're in motion."

*

We hot-toed to Robeson House. Everton and
Neville lived on the ninth floor. The lift was
covered in the tags of the South Crongton gangs.
We arrived at flat 72 and smacked the letterbox.

Terror's aunt opened the door. She had a
rocket hanging on for sweet life from her bottom
lip. She was wearing a multi-coloured headband.
Her dyed red hair tickled her waist. Freckles
orbited her green eyes. Green, white and orange
paint niced up her fingernails.

"Terry!" his aunt greeted him, hugging and
slobbering him. "What brings you round to my
parts? I haven't seen you since, what? Last
Christmas?"

"Hi, Aunty Carlene," Terror said. He wiped
his cheeks. "I got up this morning thinking that
I hadn't seen my best aunty for the longest time,
so I thought I'd wheel around to your ends to

change that. You *know* you're my fave."

"That's sweet of you," Carlene said. "My sister grew a *good* boy."

We followed Carlene into the kitchen. She fired up her rocket and took a long pull as she stirred pilchards in a bent frying pan. A pot of pasta stood next to it.

I looked through the kitchen hatch and spotted Everton and Neville playing some sort of hand-held game in the lounge. The leather sofa was nibbled at the corners – foam was coming out of it.

"How's your mum getting on with that washing machine?" Carlene asked. "The one my girlfriend sold to her?"

"It's still working," Terror replied.

"That's good," Carlene said. "The drum's got a dent in it but it should last for a while yet."

Terror nodded. "Yeah."

"How's your sis getting on with that cleaning job at the Crongton Boardwalk?" Carlene wanted to know next.

"She hasn't got the boot yet," Terror replied. "But Mum has to drag her ass outta bed most mornings. She's forever complaining about the men, the brawling and the beer smell on her trainers."

"She can complain about the men, fights and the beer smell all she wants," Carlene said. "But it'll put the bacon between your bread. A bit of cleaning wouldn't hurt your older brothers too. Way too lazy, they are."

"You're not wrong there," Terror said.

"Can I offer you boys a drink?" Carlene asked. "I've only got orange squash, otherwise it's water."

"That'll be sweet, Aunty," Terror replied. "I'm just gonna say hello to my liccle cousins."

"Maybe you can try to get them off their games," Carlene laughed. "They might listen to you."

We stepped into the lounge. Everton and Neville didn't even see us. Their eyes were locked on the game they were playing.

"Terror's here," Terror greeted them. "Cease your flow!"

Terror dropped himself on the sofa between Neville and Everton. They stopped their game and looked at him weird. I parked on a peeling armchair.

"How's my best cousins?" Terror asked.

The kids found their voices.

"Hi, Terry."

"Hi, Terry."

Terror put on his children's TV presenter smile. It freaked the funny bone outta me but it seemed to work with kids. "You know I look after you good, right?" Terror said. "Take you out to the park, buy you Captain Crunch lollies."

Everton and Neville swapped unsure glances.

"I want you to do your best cuz a big favour," Terror went on. "It would help me out big-time."

"What favour?" Everton wanted to know. He looked at Terror hard. "Are you gonna give us any pocket money for it?"

Everton was as serious as those bruvs stroking their ties as they interviewed important peeps on late-night shows.

Carlene came in with our orange squashes. "*Five* more minutes on the game," she said to Everton and Neville. "And then you can tidy up your bedroom – it's in a right state."

I sank my orange squash fast. Carlene returned to the kitchen.

"You still got the *Stars Wars* guns my mum gave you for Christmas, right?" Terror asked.

Neville picked up his game and pressed play. Everton looked at Terror.

"You know," Terror kept on. "Those Han Solo laser guns? I helped to pick 'em."

"Oh yeah," Everton remembered. "Don't know where they are."

"In your bedroom?" Terror suggested.

"Yeah." Everton nodded. "They might be in there."

"Can you get them for me?" Terror asked.

"Why d'you want 'em?" Everton asked.

"Cos ... cos ... cos ..." Terror struggled, so I cut in.

"We're doing a project at school about toys," I said. "It'll help with our homework."

"Funny homework," Everton said.

"Just *go* and get 'em." Terror raised his voice. "*Now.*"

Everton put down his controller and stood

up. He offered Terror a bad-boy eye-pass, then skipped to his room. Neville kept on playing.

We heard a lot of bang-a-ranging from Everton's room. After two curses from Carlene, Everton returned with the toy guns.

"You found 'em," Terror said.

I looked at the guns. *Han Solo laser blasters*, I thought. *The ultimate* Star Wars *experience.* I had a bad feeling about this mission.

I took a mental time-out. *We're gonna hold up a post office on Crong Broadway with* Star Wars *toy guns.* I couldn't believe this was happening.

Everton passed them on to Terror. Neville paused his game to have a look. "But that's *mine*," Neville raised his voice. "That's *my* gun. I got it for Christmas."

"But you've never played with it," Terror said. "Look! It's still in its packaging."

"I was gonna play with it tonight," Neville insisted. "It's *mine*."

Terror shot me a worried look.

"Don't bother me," Everton said. "I never wanted any stupid *Star Wars* guns in the first place. I'm too old for them."

"I *do*," Neville whined.

I dug into my pocket and found some loose change. "Can we borrow it for a few days?" I asked. "I'll pay you a liccle something now, and when I bring it back I'll give you a liccle more."

Neville thought about it. He finally nodded and said, "OK." A big grin split his cheeks.

Man! Even kids of six and eight years old in South Crong have a hard kerb-hustling thing. I handed over the coins to Neville.

"What about me?" Everton asked. "And I should get more cos I'm older. Double more."

Terror shook his head. He tunnelled into his

pockets too and came out with a few coins. He handed them to Everton.

"And when you come back you're gonna give us some more?" Everton demanded.

"Of course," Terror said. "You can trust me to the max on that one."

Everton and Neville looked like they weren't sure they could trust Terror, but they didn't say anything. Terror sank the rest of his drink and prepared to leave. "We'll catch up later," Terror said. "Make sure you're good at school."

Neville and Everton didn't reply – they were back on their game.

Carlene gave us a plastic bag for the toy guns and hugged me goodbye – her rocket smoke sent me almost as high as the twentieth floor. She kissed Terror on the cheek again. "You have to leave so early? You're not staying for dinner? We've got plenty of pasta. I can open another tin of pilchards – it won't take long to heat up."

I didn't fancy pilchards, pasta and rocket ash.

"Gotta make a move," Terror said. "Gotta start homework. I don't want my teachers blistering my ears if I don't finish it."

"That's good, that's good," Carlene said. She pulled hard on her rocket again. "A great attitude. I hope my two boys grow up like you guys."

I hoped they wouldn't.

I stepped into the lift, shaking my head. Terror ripped the guns from their packaging. I checked them out, giving them a serious eye. "They're too shiny," I said. "We can't hold up anything with these! We'll blind the person at the counter. We'll have to step in there wearing sunglasses over our masks."

Terror snatched the guns from me and looked them over like they were 22-carat diamonds.

"You're not wrong," Terror said. "But no worries. At lunchtime tomorrow we'll take them into the art room and paint 'em blackey-grey."

"*Paint 'em blackey-grey*," I repeated. "I'm not stepping into any post office with sticky painted guns. All the feds will have to do is follow the drip-drip."

"They'll be dry by the time of the mission," Terror said. "So stop bashing the buzz and get down with it."

"So when's the mission?" I wanted to know.

"Er ... in a couple days or so."

CHAPTER FIVE

Dad's Suspicious Mind

Terror and I made our way back to the south ends of
South Crongton estate. He lived in Eldridge House
and I lived in the slab opposite, Anbessa House. By
Caldonia's ranking, I must be a kerb-stain boy too.

"Remember what Caldonia said, Briggy,"
Terror reminded me. "We're linking at
Dagthorn's at nine on the bang. *Don't* be late."

"Who's in charge of this mission?" I asked.
"Caldonia or you?"

Terror grinned, flashing his molars. "Me, innit."

"Nine on the bang," I said.

Terror marched to his slab, the bag with the
Star Wars guns inside knocking against his thigh.

*

I wasn't looking forward to stepping home. The lift in Anbessa House made a weird echoing sound as I made my way to the eighth floor. I lived at number 57. The fam at number 53 had been booted out and now there was a metal grille fixed over the front door. *I hope we don't get dragon pill addicts to replace them. They're always banging on our gates begging for funds and crumbs.* I pushed my key into the lock. As soon as I landed on home tiles, Dad was in my face.

"Has your mum called you?" Dad barked. "She's meant to finish work at one but I can't get hold of her."

"Maybe she's doing overtime," I replied.

I made my way into the kitchen and Dad followed me. I opened the bread bin and, hallelujah, there were five slices of bread left. I took out two slices and dropped them in the toaster. The washing-up pile in the sink had grown.

Dad parked himself on a kitchen stool and folded his arms. He looked like he hadn't been tickled since Bible times. I sniffed the smell of toasting bread. "She always lets me know when she's doing overtime," Dad said. "Why hasn't she texted me? She always texts me if something's up."

I had the vibe that Dad had been obsessing about this since one o'clock. I tried to simmer him down. "I dunno, Dad. Maybe she's gone shopping."

I opened the fridge. There was some margarine still there – not much but enough to nice up my toast.

"She goes shopping on a *Monday*," Dad said. "Never on a Wednesday. And she would've called me if she had gone shopping."

"Like I said," I told him. "She's probably doing overtime and she's too busy to call."

"Hmmm," Dad grunted.

"What does that mean?" I asked.

Dad stood up. "You know what it is, don't you, Capleton?"

"No, Dad, I don't know what it is. Take the rabbit outta the hat on that one."

Dad paused for a long second. "It's her boss," he said in raised tones. "Mr Randall friggin Cassidy. He's got a ting for her."

"Dad, you're being—"

"I'm telling you, Cassidy *has*." Dad snapped my flow. "How d'you think she got the job in the first place?"

"Because Mum's good at meeting peeps with a smile, can count change and knows her custard tarts from her cocoa bread."

"*No*." Dad shook his head. "Cassidy's hitting on her. It's blatant. And he's married! His wife works for the council and they've got a son called Kiran – he goes to your school. Think about it.

Your mum works till three, so how comes she's not reaching home till five these days? It only takes twenty minutes to walk from the bakery to our flat. What's she up to in all that time? Eh?"

"Dad, you're being paranoid," I said. "Don't stress Mum about it when she gets home. You know what happened last time."

"*That* wasn't my fault," Dad protested.

"Mum went to Aunt Nancy's for two days—" I began.

"Yes, I know," Dad said. "You don't have to remind me. I hate it that Aunt Nancy knows all about our business. And she broadcasts it at the hairdresser's to anyone who wants to listen."

Dad wasn't lying. Aunt Nancy could take half an hour to tell you how her weaved-up hair didn't look quite on point.

"What d'you expect?" I said. "They're sisters."

The toast popped out. I put the slices on a

plate, buttered them and took them to my room.
I closed the door, not wanting to hear any more
of Dad's bitching about Mum's timekeeping. It
was happening on the regular and was starting to
vex my stress cells.

I greeted my poster of Ma Long, the Olympic
table tennis champion who watched over my bed.
"I've had a mad day, Ma."

I'd almost finished my toast when Dad
gate-crashed my room. *He never knocks.*

"Sorry to hit you with all that stuff about
Mum," he said. He glanced at his phone again.
It was five-thirty. "You're right, I'm being
paranoid," Dad continued. "She's probably
gone shopping and has her phone on silent or
something. Or her phone could be in the bottom
of her handbag. You know what she's like."

I nodded. "Yeah, I know what Mum's like."

"So how was your day?" Dad asked.

I didn't wanna tell him about my detention. But somewhere, in the corner of my brain, I did want to spill about our mission to rob the post office. Dad would put a fat full stop to it and I'd be grounded till world peace was declared, but at least it would be over. But then Terror would spit me out like a sizzling chilli. He was the only proper bredren I had. I didn't wanna let Terror down or look like a pussy in front of Caldonia.

So I told Dad, "Same old teachers, same old classes, same old issues with algebra. How about your day?"

"Went down the job centre," Dad replied. "Had a walk in ..."

He didn't reach the full stop in his sentence. Instead, he shook his head.

I'm not gonna lie, sometimes I felt sorry for Dad. The last few months, it felt like I was spending more time boosting him up than he did for me. When I was liccle, he would take me and Kingsley on trips out of the ends in his beat-up Fiesta. The engine would beg for mercy, but I loved that ride, even if Kingsley never did let me sit in the front. Dad would roll into a fish-and-chip shop near a beach and say, "*I want cod and chips twice for my boys and don't forget the slices of lemon.*" I loved the way he said *my boys*. It made me feel special.

*

Half an hour later, Mum clip-clopped over home tiles holding boxes of pizza. I helped her carry them into the kitchen as Dad scoped her.

"Kingsley!" Mum called. "Come for your pizza."

Kingsley came out of his room and joined us at the dinner table – at the last fam meeting, Mum made a new rule that we should sink meals together when we can. It didn't happen too often.

I went for two slices of chicken and pineapple. As usual, Kingsley jacked most of the garlic bread. Dad was very quiet.

"I've got twelve more hours next week," Kingsley said after a while. "My supervisor's on holiday."

"That's great," Mum replied, and Kingsley grinned. Mum poured herself a Coke and looked at Dad.

Dad crocodiled his slice of chicken and pineapple. His eyes never left his meal. Mum cleared her throat. Dad looked up but didn't say anything. Kingsley's face switched to a pissed-off tone.

"That's great news," Mum repeated. She tried a big smile. But it wasn't working on Dad.

Dad swallowed and looked at Kingsley hard. *I know that look*, I thought. *That's Dad's lecture look.*

"It'd be better news if you had a proper nine-to-five job," Dad said, "rather than celebrating that your boss gave you extra hours for one week. What about the week after, when your supervisor gets back from holiday? You need a *proper* job. Not no zero-hours crap. How d'you think you're gonna save anything or contribute to this family?"

Everything went tense. My throat dried out like there was a mini sandstorm going on in there. I recalled what Caldonia said earlier. Not just my ass that wasn't shit-hot, but my fam too.

I scoped my pizza like it was the most amazing piece of takeaway ever cooked. I glanced at Mum and she shook her head. Kingsley stood up. Dad went back to crocodiling his pizza.

Kingsley glared at Dad like he wanted to fling him into a pizza oven. "At ... at," Kingsley stuttered.

Dad looked up. Mum covered her mouth.

Kingsley's lips wobbled. "At ... at least that's twelve hours more than you!" he spat at Dad. "You lazy prick of a bitch!"

A piece of corn fell from Dad's mouth. His eyes swirled like he'd been knocked out. Kingsley collected his plate and hot-toed to his room with it. He slammed the door behind him. I gazed at my pizza.

"Did you hear that?" Dad said. "He ... he swore at me. That's all the thanks I get for working so hard in that damn yard and raising him—"

"You asked for that." Mum blocked Dad's rant. "What the friggin hell's wrong with you? Couldn't you have said *anything* nice? He's trying his best at that job, but oh no! You have to piss on it."

"He should be doing something better," Dad replied. "He went to college!"

"And *you* should be doing better too." Mum raised her voice.

Dad broke off a fat piece of pizza. It was all quiet on the Briggs front for five minutes. Then Dad changed the subject, asking Mum, "And why was you late home today?"

Squirrels running free at the hairdresser's. Here we go again. Ding ding, round 47.

"Why was I late?" Mum repeated. "What's this? Why don't you install a clocking-in machine by our front door? Or even better, why don't you staple a sat-nav chip into my butt so you know my whereabouts?"

"You never come home after five-thirty," Dad said, louder. "Why didn't you text me?"

"Cos I stayed on to help Randall with a delivery. Then he offered to take me around the corner for a drink to say thanks."

"It's *Randall* now, is it?" Dad replied. "No more Mr Cassidy?"

"Grow up!" Mum roared at Dad. "And there's

nothing wrong with accepting a drink from your boss after work."

Dad sprang from his seat like someone had pressed an eject button. He waved a finger at Mum. "And that's all he wants, eh?" Dad said. "Eh? Oh, I bet he wants more than drinks. I know what those kinda guys are like. Them kinda guys are always on the hunt for more women. And they don't care who they're married to."

Mum wiped her mouth with a tissue, slow and calm. This was all new. I would feel more comfortable if she launched a cuss attack. I was used to that. But she narrowed her eyes like she was planning something cold. "I work *hard* in that place," Mum said. She slapped her palm on the table. I felt the vibrations.

"I work *hard* here," Mum continued. "*Too* freaking hard. Look at this place. Have you done the laundry? No? And that washing-up in the sink hasn't been touched since I left the flat this morning. If I don't do it, fungi will start growing on it – and you still wouldn't friggin notice! So, if *Randall* offers to buy me a rum and coke after work, I'm taking it. And you're not gonna make me feel guilty!"

"He's hitting on you," Dad yelled.

"I couldn't give a sugar puff if Randall is," said Mum. "If he thinks he's getting something, then he took the wrong exit at the roundabout. But you know what, I think you're wrong. Randall is just being nice. Nice men *do* exist out there. And if *you* don't trust me, then take your lazy mitts outta my face and take your suspicions to the people at the job centre! They might listen and play a violin for ya. I *won't*."

"I might just do that!" Dad yelled back.

Mum pushed her plate of pizza away, crossed her arms and snorted like a pissed-off bull. Dad swiped the remaining garlic bread and continued eating.

It was all too awkward for me. I hot-toed to the kitchen and picked up a tray so I could sink the rest of my pizza in my room.

"Now look what you've done!" I heard Mum roar.

*

Two hours later, someone tickled my door.

"Come in," I said.

It was Mum. She sat on my bed but couldn't meet my eyes. She spoke in a near whisper. "I'm sorry you had to hear ... you know ... what went on at dinner."

"That's all right, Mum," I said. "Dad's just going on paranoid. Best to ignore him."

Mum looked up and said, "He ... he doesn't mean to. It's just that since he got made redundant, he's lost ... he's lost ..."

"I know, Mum."

"So, how was your day then?" Mum asked after a long pause.

I didn't wanna make her day worse by spilling info about my detention. I still had the post office mission nibbling away in the corner of my mind. *We can't do it. But, if Terror drops me as his best bredren, I'll be on my lonesome. Things haven't been too good between Terror and me since Caldonia wriggled her butt into his life. Maybe at the end of this mission we'll be tight again. Best bredrens.*

"It was good, you know," I told Mum. "Had English and PE. Still don't get algebra."

Mum chuckled. "Nor did I. Any homework?"

"Just revision," I replied.

"Make sure you do it," Mum said, and pointed at me. "You've got those SATs tests coming up."

*

I was in the middle of reading something about the First World War when Kingsley bounced into my room. Like Mum and Dad, he never knocked. Kingsley closed the door behind him and crashed on my bed. If I did that in his room, he'd boot my long butt out.

"I can't wait to fly from here," Kingsley said. "As soon as I save up the funds, I'm gone. And I'm not gonna come back till he's gone."

"You're still brewing over Dad," I said. "You know what he's like. Don't worry yourself about it."

"It's not just cos of that," Kingsley insisted. "It's now like twenty-four-seven that Mum and Dad are cursing the tonsils outta each other. I can't take their dramas any more."

"At least you can fly," I said. "What can I do? I'm stuck here. When you're not here, I've gotta be the referee to their warring."

Kingsley sat up and spoke in a whisper. "You can move in with me when I'm set up," he said.

"Move in with you?" I repeated. "Stop playing! I've still got the bruises after borrowing your tracksuit bottoms for school."

"No, I'm serious," Kingsley said. "How long has this been going on for?"

"I'm not counting the days," I replied.

"Almost a year," Kingsley answered his own question. "Since Dad lost his job at the timber yard."

"That was rough," I said. "He'd been working there for the longest time." I remembered how he'd let me pick out the splinters in his fingers when I was liccle.

"But that's no excuse for Dad to take out his shit on Mum," Kingsley said. "She went out and got herself a job. I dunno why she puts up with him. I told her to sack his grumpy ass. She'd be happier on her own."

"Don't get involved, Kingsley," I said. "Leave 'em to work it out."

Kingsley stood up and shook his head. "It's not gonna be worked out, bruv. It's going downhill on a cement truck with its brakes not working. I hope they just write a full stop to all this shit, sign the divorce papers and press the reboot button."

Mum and Dad, divorce? I searched Kingsley's eyes. He was as serious as I'd ever seen him.

"The offer's there, Capleton, when I make the move," Kingsley said. "You don't deserve to live in this drama every freaking day."

Kingsley opened the door. Before he left, he added, "Think about it."

I thought about it all night.

CHAPTER SIX

Reconnaissance

Next morning, I had a breakfast of one Weetabix and a dribble of milk. Every time Mum and Dad got caught up in something, Dad went on strike and didn't do shit around the house. The flat was quiet. Mum was asleep, Dad had stepped out early on a job hunt and Kingsley had marched to work. I washed up the mountain of stuff in the sink. I was thinking about bouncing straight to school, but if I didn't turn up at Dagthorn's, Terror would never forgive me. I didn't want Terror branding me a mouse – or any other rodent – for the rest of my days.

I zipped up my school bag and headed to the

front door. Mum stepped in front of me. She was wearing her basketball shorts and a baggy Tupac T-shirt – her sleeping garms. I could see she'd been crying.

"Gimme a hug," Mum said.

"What's wrong, Mum?" I asked.

"Just gimme a hug," she repeated.

We embraced, and she wouldn't let me go for the longest time. She finally released me and mopped her eyes.

I didn't know what to say to make her feel any better. "Mum, I gotta step," I came up with. "I'm gonna be late for school."

I hated lying to her.

"OK," Mum said. "Be good."

She gave me a weak smile as I left. *Maybe she's thinking about the big D – divorce*, I thought. I wondered what tiles Dad would land his toes on if she divorced him – he didn't have any fam in Crongton. As far as I knew, all he had was an older bruv living in Biggin Spires. Dad didn't spill too much about him.

I had time to kill, so instead of waiting for the lift, I bounced down the staircase. I took my tie and my blazer off and stuffed them into my bag. I reached Dagthorn's at 8.40 a.m. The sun blazed down and I remembered I'd forgotten to bless my armpits. *Knowing my luck, Caldonia Lake will be the first to sniff me out.*

The sensible, level voice in my head told my long ass to burn my soles to school. But I didn't listen to it. Instead, I bought a packet of extra-strong mints. I'd sucked the mintyness outta three of them by the time I spotted Terror. A big grin sliced his cheeks.

"You reached, Briggy," he greeted.

"And?" I replied. "Did you think I'd mouse out?"

We sat on the low wall outside Dagthorn's

and I offered him a mint. He took two.

"What time does the post office open?" I asked.

"Nine, I think," Terror replied.

"So why are we stepping there today if we haven't got the guns sorted yet?" I whispered.

"It's like we said yesterday," Terror said. "We have to know the shakedown of the place before we make the strike."

"Caldonia might not even turn up," I said. "You know what, if she doesn't reach by nine-fifteen, I'm rolling to school."

"She'll come, Briggy," Terror assured me. "She's on it."

Caldonia did come. Nine o'clock on the bang. Her hair was in ponytails and blue lipstick sexed up her mouth. Her shoes were blistered and her black leggings had holes in them, but she still looked as sexy as Beyoncé.

"You bruvs ready?" Caldonia asked.

Terror shot up to his feet like a missile was chasing his butt. "Yep," he said. "Let's do this."

"Before we go," I said. "Aren't you gonna take off your blazers and ties? We don't want them to recognise us by our uniforms, do we?"

Terror and Caldonia thought about it.

"Briggs, you're not as dumb as you look," Caldonia said.

I didn't love her joke but I smiled anyway. Caldonia and Terror took off their blazers and ties and packed them into their rucksacks.

"We got the guns," said Terror.

Caldonia's eyes doubled in size and she demanded, "Let's have a look."

Terror took off his rucksack and passed it on to Caldonia.

Caldonia looked inside. She chomped her top lip. "Not bad, not bad," she said. "A bit shiny, but we can work on that."

"We're gonna paint 'em blackey-grey in the art room," Terror said.

Fifteen minutes later, we were on Crong Broadway. The traffic was thick and the 159 bus was corked. We rolled past the Falcon Bank and then Lovindeer's Lounge Bar. Outside, a greyback with a limp swept the floor. Three crusty guys – wearing white helmets and cockroach stomper boots – sank scrambled eggs on toast in Barrington's Hollywood Diner. Gloria Grahame's Tanning Salon hadn't opened yet. I scoped the paintings in the art gallery next door, but they were a mystery to me. Caldonia was suffering from chronic munchies, so we stepped into a Tesco Extra store. She felt the need to feed on bourbons. She gave us two biscuits each.

The post office was at the end of the street.

As we neared it, my insides scratched and churned like a DJ was mixing them. I checked that

Terror still had his rucksack fixed to his back. I hoped today really was a scouting mission and he wouldn't do anything cadazy this morning. Caldonia led the way up the four steps to the entrance.

There were six counters but only three were open. Two of the counter staff were women and the other was an older bruv with a shinehead. He was wearing a V-neck pullover and a polka-dot bow tie. One customer was counting her euro Gs. There was a passport photo booth in the corner. About twelve peeps were waiting in a neat line. Most of them were carrying parcels.

"We can't just block here and scope out the place," I whispered. "We look like fugitives."

"Speak for yourself," Terror said. "The only one looking like a fugitive is your long ass."

"What does being long have to do with anything?" I argued. "Can't short people look dodgy too?"

"Will you two simmer down?" Caldonia cut in. "Briggs isn't wrong. We gotta act normal."

I grinned an *I'm-up-to-spec-on-this-mission-more-than-you* grin. Caldonia nudged me and said, "Go and buy a stamp from that machine while we check the exits. Buying stamps is standard in a post office."

There was a stamp machine in another corner.

"Me? I haven't got the funds to buy a stamp," I said.

"Nor have I," Terror admitted. "My liccle hustler cuz, Everton, took the funds I had."

"Oh, some pissing pennies for a frucking horse!" Caldonia swore. She dug into her purse and pulled out some coins. "Get a second-class one."

I hot-toed over to the stamp machine. I felt as if the whole world and its great-grandma was scoping my lanky ass, even though I wasn't doing anything wrong. I bought the stamp and rejoined the others.

"D'you want it?" I said, and offered the stamp to Caldonia.

"Who am I gonna send a frigging letter to?" she said. "Keep it."

I banked the stamp in my back pocket.

"OK," Caldonia said. "Let's step out and run down this mission line by line."

We didn't say anything until we were halfway down Blowhawk Lane – a liccle road that led to the back of the shops. I couldn't deny it – the sniff of notes in the post office had teased the shopping sprees outta me. I thought of Dr Dre headphones and one of them Sekonda watches, thick as a brick, to glam up my wrist.

"We can do this," Caldonia said. "There are just three people on the counters and two of 'em are women. Plus the shinehead in the bow tie looks like he couldn't catch an old turtle."

"I'm with you, Caldonia," Terror agreed. But then he'd be with her if she planned to break into Donald Trump's toilet. "But how are we gonna drop this?" Terror asked. "Should all of us bounce up to the counter or should it just be me?"

"Hold up a sec," I said. "Don't they have buzzers under the counter that sound off at the fed station if they press them? I don't want a swarm of blue bloods scoping my forehead with their AK-47s. And you know how eager they are with the trigger."

"It's a *post office*," Terror said. "They don't have them buzzers in post offices. Trust me on that one."

"How do you know?" I asked. "How many post offices have you jacked in the last week?"

"Typical Briggs," Caldonia said. "Always dropping a fatberg to block our flow."

"I'm *not* blocking your flow," I protested. "Every post office has them buzzers."

"They want you to *think* they have those buzzers," Terror said. "But they don't. Briggy, it's gonna be easy-licious, so quit browning your boxers on this one. Did you see how many Gs that woman was counting?"

Caldonia licked her lips. Man. I wished she wouldn't do that. "About five hundred euros I reckon," she said.

"*That's* the counter we're gonna jack," said Terror. "The foreign-money one. And we're gonna be counting wad after wad."

"But if we get wadfuls of euros and dollars," I said, "how are we gonna change 'em into pounds? We can't take 'em back to the post office."

"We'll change 'em at a bank," Caldonia suggested.

"Don't you need a bank account to change Gs at a bank?" I asked.

"I think you do," Terror said. "And I haven't got a bank account. I haven't even got a piggy bank."

"Nor have I," I said. "My mum keeps her notes under her bed but the only thing that's under my mattress is dust."

"Eeeewwww!" Caldonia said, and pulled a face. "Have you ever heard of a hoover?"

I let that one pass.

CHAPTER SEVEN

Arts and Crafts

We rolled back up Blowhawk Lane and turned onto Crongton Broadway. Caldonia chewed on the bourbons, deep in thought. The traffic was still dense. It wasn't until we passed Gloria Grahame's tanning salon that Caldonia broke the silence. "I've got a savings account," she admitted. "I've only got a few shiny ones in it, but it means I can roll up to the counter and change some foreign Gs."

"Problem solved!" Terror said. "We'll lick the euro counter."

He moved in for a kiss but Caldonia backed away and slapped his forehead. "Retreat!" she snapped. "I've still got biscuit crumbs in my mouth."

We set off for school. I still couldn't get the Dr Dre headphones outta my mind. I dreamed of flexing my toes on a patch of green somewhere and listening to a mixtape by Early B or Soprano Blender.

We stopped off in Crongton Park and Caldonia fired up half a rocket. She took six pulls before passing it on to Terror. "Take it down slow," Caldonia warned. "This shit is potent. You don't wanna see funky unicorns and hear talking frogs during History."

We finally rolled by the school gates. "So, when's zero hour?" I asked.

Terror killed his stride. He wasn't looking too steady on his toes. *It's a good thing he's not walking the beam in gym today*, I thought. "Tomorrow," Terror said. "We'll do what we did today – link at Dagthorn's at nine on the bang."

"Tomorrow?" I repeated. "I've got PE in the morning."

"Yeah," Terror said. "I think they'll survive without you. It's basketball and no one has ever been as long as you but so shit at b-ball."

That stung but Terror wasn't lying.

Caldonia shook her head and put on a squeaky voice. *"I've got PE in the morning,"* she mimicked me. "Are you *on* this or not? I wanna solid confirmation!"

Caldonia and Terror both scoped me hard. "Of course I'm on it," I insisted.

"Then *act* like it," Caldonia said.

"OK, all good," Terror said. "Briggy, we'll link in the art room to paint the guns."

"What time?" I asked.

"One o'clock."

"On the bang," Caldonia added.

"Have you got something about bangs?" I said. "Do you love popping balloons in your spare time?"

Caldonia gave me a long side-eye.

*

We were late for school of course, so we had to report to reception. They fell for our fake news: Caldonia felt sick with period cramps, so Terror and me walked her to the pill store to get painkillers. They didn't write our names down in the latecomers' book and Mr Holman even gave Terror and me ratings for *showing concern for another student.*

I had History and English before lunch. Jennifer Caltrao was in my English class and I think I spent most of it studying her long sleeky black hair. When I wasn't doing that, I scoped her curvylicious bod. I managed to swap a word with her when class was dismissed.

"Do ... do ... d'you get it?" I stuttered.

The hotel scene in *Straight Outta Compton* crashed into my mind.

"Get what?" Jennifer said in her kissable Portuguese tones.

"The book we're reading," I said. "*Of Mice and Men.*"

"Finding it difficult," Jennifer replied.

"Me too," I said, and nodded.

Then Jennifer was gone. At least I had graduated from saying hi to making a four-sentence convo with her.

I made it to the art room just before one. Paintings of tall slabs, jagged knives and crying mums were Blu-tacked to the walls. Terror and Caldonia were already there. They had put Han Solo's laser blasters on sheets of newspaper. I wondered what Everton and Neville would make of their guns' new colours. Terror had an oversize apron on and was wearing blue surgical gloves. Blackey-grey paint arched his left eyebrow. He looked ridiculous but I killed my chuckles.

"I thought you were gonna paint the guns," I said. "Not perform surgery on them."

That even made Caldonia laugh.

Terror ignored me, focused his eyes and worked on the guns like he was painting the follow-up to the *Mona Lisa*.

I couldn't lie – they looked more like the blazing deal than before.

We heard footsteps and spun around. Ms Rees, the head of art, stomped into the art room. She heavy-heeled towards us in her blue Dr Marten boots, diversity headscarf, a paint-sploshed baggy T-shirt and earrings the size of basketball hoops.

"What are you doing over there?" she wanted to know. "Don't you know it's lunchtime?"

I froze. None of us answered. Terror's eyes did this looking-here and looking-there panic thing. Caldonia stayed as cool as a chocolate mousse in an igloo's fridge.

Ms Rees took a closer look at the blackey-grey guns. I saw a fat question mark form in the gap between her tattooed eyebrows. She put her hands on her hips. A piece of clay clogged up her left ear.

"Explanation?" Ms Rees demanded.

Terror stuttered. Caldonia just gazed into space and twirled her hair.

"It's for our nephews," I said. "You see, they've got four toy guns between 'em, and they're the same colour – black. So we thought we'd paint two of 'em so they know which two belong to who."

"I see," Ms Rees said, and nodded. "But this is *my* art room and you're using *my* paint. Next time, *ask* first."

"Yes, Ms Rees," I replied. "I was going to but you weren't around."

"Hmmm," Ms Rees snorted. "Make sure you wash the brushes and leave the working space exactly how you found it."

Terror found his voice. "Yeah, we're on that," he said. "Briggy's gonna do that right now."

Ms Rees collected something from her office, which was inside the studio, then locked the office door and hoofed her way out.

"Why do *I* have to clean up?" I protested.

"Cos you were the last one to reach," Caldonia replied. "*I* mixed the paint."

Terror found a space on the radiator at the back of the classroom to dry the guns. He washed his hands in a sink. Caldonia yanked him into a hug and sizzled his lips with a kiss. She side-eyed me as they pressed the saliva outta each other. My cheeks burned with envy.

"Link us after last bell," Caldonia said, after she came up for air. "We'll run down the mission one last time."

"Where?" I said.

Caldonia thought about it. "By the school gates, innit."

There was no question she was in charge of this mission. "OK, I'll be there," I said.

"*Don't* get detention," Terror warned.

They rolled out of the room and left me on my lonesome. As I washed the brushes, I thought of lip-smacking Jennifer Caltrao, just like Terror had done with Caldonia. *After that four-sentence convo, at least Jennifer knows I'm breathing. Maybe next time I'll ask her if she likes jacking post offices – I might get a kiss outta it.*

*

I didn't get detention but Terror did.

In his Maths class, he got into a mad feud with Evelyn Campbell. I heard that Evelyn started it by calling Terror a ginger troll who lived under the grimiest bridge in the world. It ended up with Terror branding Evelyn's mum the ghost whore of South Crong. Evelyn took off her shoe and tried to clong the bogey outta Terror's nose.

Caldonia and I waited on a bench in the playground. She had parked on one end and I was at the other.

"Why won't you let Terror come to your gates?" I asked.

"What's it to you?" Caldonia snapped.

"He's really on you."

"Yeah, I know."

"He's got the love bug bad," I added.

"Love?" Caldonia replied. "Maybe he feels that way now but tomorrow he might hate the living sight of me."

"Why d'you say that?" I asked.

Caldonia scoped the concrete for a long second before she answered. "Cos fam and peeps you love have the power to hurt you," she said.

"So you don't think it's gonna be a long-term ting?" I asked.

"What's it to you?" Caldonia barked again. "Instead of quizzing me, you should be thinking about how you're gonna get on the field with Jennifer Caltrao."

"You know about that?" I asked.

Caldonia nodded. "I've seen you microscoping her bod in school – with your tongue so far out it licks your laces."

I tried a different tone and asked, "Have you got any bruvs or sisters?"

She looked up and stared into space. "No," she finally replied.

"I've got an older bruv," I offered.

She turned to look at me and raised her fist as if she was celebrating. "Well, goodooly-hoo for you!"

"D'you get on with your fam?" I asked.

Caldonia thought about it. I sensed a liccle touch of sadness in her eyes. Her tone softened as she said, "It's a long story. It's not pretty."

"You can say, if you want," I told her. "My parents are going ..."

Caldonia stood up as Terror emerged from the school building. She hugged him till his ribs creaked and for the next sixty seconds I had to watch them smacking the saliva from each other's tongues. Jealousy flamed my cheeks once again. Caldonia finally pulled away. "Next time you get detention, you're not getting treats," Caldonia said to Terror.

"Sorry," Terror replied.

"We have to run down the programme for the

morning," I cut in. "Everyone's gotta be on point."

Terror leaned in again to kiss Caldonia but she backed away. I couldn't kill my smirk.

"I heard you launched a cuss attack on Evelyn Campbell," Caldonia said to Terror. "That stuck-up, mooncrater-nose, big-foot bitch. You should've done it outside class."

"You're not wrong," Terror replied. "But she was getting on my case. I had to offload on her."

"Good for you," Caldonia said. "I won't even use the toilets she shits in, but don't offload on her the day I tell you *not* to get a pissing detention."

"Er, excuse me," I said. "We forgot something."

"What's that?" asked Terror.

"The masks," I reminded them. "Shall we roll back to the art room and get them now? I think Ms Rees has gone—"

"No." Caldonia shook her head. "I've been thinking about it. We're gonna wear baseball caps instead."

"Baseball caps?" I repeated. "But they'll—"

"We can't just enter the post office wearing masks," Caldonia said. "We'll get clipped before we get to the freaking counter! No, burn that idea. Best to just queue up like we're on the regular and make our demands once we reach the counter. The peaks of the baseball caps will cover our faces from the CCTV."

I looked at Terror.

"Makes sense," Terror said.

"Have you got the guns?" I asked.

Terror patted his rucksack.

"Are they dry?" I said.

"Yep," Terror replied. "They're looking the real blazing deal."

Something inside my stomach dived – a proper

Tom Daley triple twist and double somersault.

We rolled out of school. Caldonia had the living munchies, so we headed towards Dagthorn's.

"We link up at Dagthorn's at nine," Terror said in a *Mission Impossible* whisper. "We come up the back way to Crong Broadway and roll up to Blowhawk Lane. We don't want peeps seeing us stepping into the post office if we can help it – from the bank, Lovindeer's Lounge Bar, the diner or anywhere else. We have to keep that to a minimum."

"I hear that," I said, nodding.

"We put on our caps when we touch down on Blowhawk Lane," Terror continued. "We tug 'em down to cover our brows. We don't want any CCTV zooming in for close-ups, so *never* look up. Then we roll into the post office and join the queue—"

"No getting distracted by the envelopes and the bubble wrap," Caldonia cut in.

"And then we step up to the euro counter," Terror went on. "Take our guns from our rucksacks and demand our Gs."

Freezing North Pole sweat dripped down my spine. I tried to put on my best *up-for-it* face but my guts and my heart were having a snow fight with each other.

"And then we set our gears to Flash speed and get our toes outta there," Terror added. "Caldonia, make sure you're wearing your trainers."

"I'm on that," she said.

"Maybe we should hire a racing car to get outta there," I quipped.

"Briggs, maybe your jokes are not too funny," Caldonia spat.

This is not gonna work, I thought. *It'll be a mad success if we even make it to the post office without Caldonia and my long self brawling.*

CHAPTER EIGHT

A Call from Aunty Carlene

We arrived at Dagthorn's. Caldonia bought another packet of bourbons. She gave Terror three and me two. I was nibbling the second one when Terror's mobile screamed. He answered it.

"Hi, Aunty Carlene," Terror said.

We stepped on as Terror nodded to whatever Aunty Carlene was telling him.

"No, we haven't finished our project yet," Terror said. "No, we still need the guns for the next couple of days ... This evening? Neville's upset? He wants to play with 'em tonight? Tell him not to fret, he'll get it back."

Caldonia and I swapped worried looks.

"Right," Terror said. "But does he really want it tonight? OK. OK then. See you later."

He killed the call as we neared Somerleyton House.

"Neville wants his gun back," Terror said. "Tonight."

"Tonight?" Caldonia repeated.

"Yep, tonight," Terror confirmed. "And what's more, Aunty Carlene said she don't mind coming around to my gates later on to get it."

"Why does Neville want his gun back tonight?" I asked. "I gave him funds so we could borrow it."

"Cos he just saw *Empire Strikes Back* on Sky Movies," Terror explained. "And he wants to play with it. Neville thinks he's a Jedi now and he wants to murk his older brother."

"Maybe Briggs didn't give him much funds," Caldonia said. "How much did you give him?"

"Plenty," I replied – I didn't reveal it was only

twenty-eight pence. "This is rubbish," I added. "The gun was in its packaging – Neville had never played with it before."

Terror shook his head. "Neville's a bit spoilt," he said. "He bawls down the block if his mum doesn't give him his Coco Pops in the morning. I shoulda gave you the intelligence on that one."

We rolled on for another minute.

"Give the guns to me," I said. "Say to Neville or your aunty Carlene that you left them at school. That works, doesn't it?"

Terror flashed his molars. Caldonia seemed to like my plan. She nodded. "Briggs, you're not as empty as you look," Caldonia said.

I let that one go.

Larkhall House shadowed us when Caldonia stepped off. On the third floor, a wife versus husband cursing match was booting off.

"Can't I stroll with you to your gates?" Terror

asked Caldonia. "It's gonna be tense tomorrow."

Caldonia glanced back to us. "We can release all the tension when the mission's done," she said with a smile. "Save it all for then, bootykoos."

Bootykoos? Jealousy fly-kicked my lean ass.

Then she was gone. We watched her rock that bootykoo behind of hers until she stepped beyond Drockwell House.

"Why don't you just follow her?" I suggested.

"Nah," Terror replied. "She won't love that. But I'll land my toes on her home tiles one day and I'll find out what colour her pillow slips are, the brand of her lipstick and the names of all her dolls. Trust me on that."

"I don't think a chick like Caldonia has ever played with dolls," I said.

"She did," Terror said. "Her paps bought 'em for her and now she's grown she doesn't want to fling 'em away."

Terror was quiet as we hot-stepped back to our ends. I just couldn't delete the thought of Caldonia playing with dolls from my mind. I was about to bounce up to my slab but Terror held my arm. "You've got the arms, Briggy. *Don't* forget 'em."

"That's not an option," I replied.

"You're gonna have my spine on this one?" Terror asked.

"You're my bredren from kneecap-high," I assured him. We crashed fists. "I'm on this," I added. "I'll never let you down."

"I know you won't," Terror said.

"We're ... we're not gonna hurt anyone, are we?" I said.

"What?" Terror replied. "Are you cadazy? With *Star Wars* guns? No one's gonna get blazed, Briggy."

CHAPTER NINE

Dad Gone Ghost

I landed on home tiles, where I found Mum stirring onions, peppers and mince in a frying pan. She was listening to some old-school soul music that pumped out from a Bluetooth speaker on a shelf. I parked myself on a stool.

"You feeling better, Mum?" I asked.

Mum placed the wooden spoon on a plate and ran her fingers in my curls. "Much better," she said. "Tings will work out."

"How will things work out, Mum? Dad was frothing last night. This is happening all too reg—"

"I'll let you know in time," Mum cut me off.

"Not just yet. Now, do whatever homework you have to do and let me put the rice on."

"Where's Dad?" I asked.

Mum took her time in answering. She picked up the wooden spoon and went back to stirring. "He's about somewhere," she said.

"Where?" I pushed again.

"Probably job-hunting."

I poured myself a glass of water. I sank half of it and looked at Mum again. "Are you two in the talking zone?" I asked.

Mum carried on stirring the food. She didn't turn around to look at me but said, "We'll talk later, Capleton. Let me finish cooking – Kingsley will be home soon."

We sat down for dinner when Kingsley had reached home. Dad's place was empty. I could see the stress in Mum's eyes as she guillotined a long stick of garlic bread. I think she knew where

Dad was but she wasn't leaking. I wanted a calm evening, so I didn't try to raise that beast from the lagoon.

Kingsley was spilling about his lazy boss who was always chatting on her mobile and had it gummed to her ear for most of the day. Mum topped up her glass of red wine and sank that instead of eating anything. She tried to smile a couple of times but it didn't reach her eyes. The tension was so thick the *Texas Chainsaw Massacre* bruv would've had trouble slicing it.

When I finished the washing-up, I hot-toed to my room. I nodded at Ma Long and told him, "I've had an insane day."

Kingsley barged into my room just as I was hunting for my Dallas Cowboys baseball cap. As usual, Kingsley crashed onto my bed. "I know you're feeling it, bruv," he said. "We all are. But Mum will chat to us on the level in the next day or so."

"Why can't she chat to us now?" I asked.

"Just give her time," Kingsley said. "And try to do all the things you always do. Like taking out the rubbish, doing the washing-up and your homework."

I found my Dallas Cowboys cap in the corner of my wardrobe. It was a bit dusty. I tried it on for size, then squeezed it into my school bag. "How am I s'posed to focus on any homework with all this drama going on?" I asked.

"I'd thought you'd wanna do some revision," Kingsley said. "It'll keep your mind off thinking about our situation. And our situation's grim, bruv."

"Is Mum gonna boot Dad to the kerb?" I wanted to know.

Kingsley didn't answer. Instead, he sat up, grabbed my bag and emptied its contents all over my bed. My heart sent drum messages to my ribs. "If you want, I'll help you with something,"

Kingsley offered. "Mum said you were having issues with your algebra …"

My bruv's gaze was distracted by Han Solo's two blackey-grey laser guns. To my eyes, they had grown into machine guns that the Expendables might have used.

"What's this?" Kingsley asked. He picked them up and examined them. "You're a bit old to play gangsters and blue bloods, bruv."

My ribs sent pulses to the rest of my body. "Just … just toy guns," I managed.

"What the freaking bells are you doing with toy guns?" Kingsley asked. He dropped them on the bed again.

I tried to think fast but my brain was on a go-slow.

"What's the matter with you, Capleton?" my bruv said, his voice raised. "Don't you know the blue bloods can smoke you away if they see you with these? They'll say they thought it was an AK-47 or something and they had to protect themselves. They'll say you were chanting *Armageddon* and end-of-the-world shit. There'll be brothers marching outside Crongton fed station chanting *Black Lives Matter*. But you won't hear that – cos your squiddly butt will be in a coffin. And it'll be a closed casket, cos the sight of your blazed ass won't be pretty. You better fling these in the rubbish chute."

"They're not mine to fling away," I said.

"Then whose are they?" Kingsley asked.

"Terror's," I replied.

"You're still calling *Terry Forbes* Terror? You wanna drop that."

"He loves being called Terror," I said.

"He needs to downsize his ego," Kingsley said. "Anyways, you're *not* stepping out of this yard with these toy guns."

"We only painted them for Terror's cousins – Everton and Neville."

Kingsley gave me a Judge Dredd glare. "I told you already, Terry's a bad vibe on you. He's always getting his ginger ass into trouble and his fam are no better – you know his uncle's a villain and a half, right? Fergus Forbes. He'd jack the doorknob outta an empty room. Fergus is still counting bricks in Drumfort prison. Crookery's in his DNA."

"You can't blame Terror for that," I said. "Fergus has been in and out of jail since I was nine years old."

"All the same, the Forbes are all crooks," Kingsley insisted. "They've got the addresses of four prisons on their sat navs. Why don't you find some new bredrens?"

"Cos peeps laugh at me at school," I said. "*Look at Lurch! The longest boy in South Crong but he can't even shoot a hoop all day long! Tell me what the weather's like up there! Can I put a satellite on your head!* I hear it every day."

"How many times do I have to tell you to ignore them haters?" Kingsley said. "Don't pay them any mind."

I put the toy guns back inside my bag. "Terror doesn't take the living piss outta me," I said. "He's had my spine for the longest time."

Kingsley shook his head. "At least *try* to find some new bredrens," he said. "It's not good just to have one. What about table tennis? You're top ranking at that. Didn't you google the table tennis clubs in our ends?"

"Yeah, I did," I replied. "But the nearest one is in Notre Dame. I'm not stepping up to those postcodes, not with the Hunchbacker crew. They don't love South Crong peeps. In fact, no one outside these ends loves South Crongtonians."

Kingsley stood up and said, "I hear you on that one. OK, take those toy guns back to Terry's cousins but *don't* take 'em out in public."

He left as I picked up my books and placed them in my school bag.

I reconsidered the mission. The idea of serving Jennifer Caltrao the best cheesecake in the house seemed a million miles away. I promised Terror I wouldn't let him down. *Crongton isn't like the United murking fields of America, where everyone and their hamster's got a rocket launcher. There's no chance of someone blazing me away in a post office in the UK.* But it was kinda spooky to think about someone firing lead into me.

To sweeten up my mood I switched on my laptop and watched Ma Long's best table tennis rallies on YouTube. It wasn't even debateable. Ma Long was G.O.A.T. – the greatest of all time.

I zonked out for a while. When I woke up again, I found my PC had timed out and my bedroom light was switched off. I checked the time – 2.20 a.m.

Was Dad back? I got up and slapped my parents' bedroom door. No one answered. I stood there for two minutes, not sure of what to do. I just had to check if Dad had bounced home. I didn't want my parents' marriage blitzed. I smacked the door again.

"Who is it?" Mum asked.

"Me," I said. "Capleton."

"What d'you want? It's nearly half two in the morning."

I went into the bedroom. Mum had switched on her night-lamp. A cookbook and Mum's reading glasses were resting on her bedside table. The side next to her was empty. No Dad.

"I ... I just wondered ... where's Dad?" I asked.

"Capleton, it's very late," Mum said. "I have to be at work by half six in the morning. We've got a delivery at the bakery. We'll talk tomorrow. Now, go back to bed."

"But—" I began.

"*Bed*," Mum insisted.

I returned to my room but I knew something was off-key. I had a vibe that Mum wasn't telling me the full story. But I had to try to let that one go for now, cos tomorrow was zero hour. No matter what, I couldn't let Terror down. Yet if the mission went all wrong, it might be just Mum and Kingsley sleeping in our yard tomorrow night.

CHAPTER TEN

The Day of the Mission

The flat was empty when I got up at 6.40 a.m.

I sank three Weetabix with a generous dose of milk – Mum had gone shopping yesterday. I washed up everything in the sink and even gave my room a hoovering. I took a shower and polished my molars. I gazed into the mirror above the sink and thought of what Kingsley had said last night. *Find new bredrens*, he'd advised.

But Terror was the one who had my spine. Like on the second day in year seven, when the whole PE class were calling me *Highslab*. When I sat on my own, he'd been the only one to park next to me. "*Don't* let the cuss bruvs get to you,"

Terror had said. "Have you ever seen a rom-com where the chick smacks lips with a mini-me? It never happens, bruv! Princess Leia never bent tongues with an Ewok, did she? Usain Bolt probably had all of your issues but now he drives Grand Prix brand cars, dances with fit chicks at carnivals and gives funds to the school he was at."

No, I can't mouse outta the mission now, I told myself.

Before I left the flat, I checked that the blackey-grey guns were still in my school bag. They were. My Dallas Cowboys baseball cap was there too.

I left at 8.35 a.m. The lift took its time coming. When it did, there were seven people in it, including Patricia James and her nine-month-old baby, Christopher. Christopher wasn't having a blessed morning. He spat out his dummy and bawled down the block. His screaming scraped my nerves.

A stiff rain fell outside. Pure greyness filled the heavens. I took out my cap and pulled it on.

I trekked to Dagthorn's and parked on the low wall outside. Puddles surrounded my feet. My backside got wet, but I didn't care. 8.45 a.m.

Nerves twanged inside of me, so I bought some extra-strong mints to suck on. I had sunk five mints by the time Terror arrived. My breath was fresher than a polar bear's. 9.01 a.m.

"Are you ready, Briggy?" Terror asked.

"Of course," I lied.

"We're gonna make some serious Gs," Terror said. He had the look of an eight-year-old kid who had just been given his first smartphone.

"Where's Caldonia?" I asked.

I prayed to the Crongton gods that she wouldn't turn up.

"She just texted me," Terror said. "Her toes are in motion – she's on the road."

Two minutes later, Caldonia arrived. A black umbrella kept her long curly hair dry. She was wearing black lipstick and brown eyeliner. *Simply gorgylicious.*

"Blazers and ties *off*," Caldonia ordered.

Terror and I did as we were told.

"It's good that it's pissing down in anger," Caldonia said. "It'll put off a few greybacks from coming out and corking up the post office."

"Anything will help," I said. "The post office is normally ram-jammed first thing in the morning. But I s'pose we can't leave it too late, cos Mr Holman might call our parents."

"You're not wrong there," said Caldonia.

I passed on one of the guns to Terror. He banked it in his rucksack and pulled on his cap. We searched each other's eyes.

"Are we in gear?" Terror asked.

I nodded. "Yep. Been in gear since I got up this morning."

"Then let's step," Caldonia said.

She linked arms with Terror, held the umbrella over their heads and we rolled.

We took a time-out in Crongton Park. Caldonia fired up a rocket. She pulled on it five times, then handed it over to Terror. Terror blew smoke rings. Then he looked at me for a long second and passed me the rocket. I didn't take it.

"Go on, Briggs," Caldonia urged me on. "It'll cool down your nerves. You can't be a rocket virgin for the rest of your days."

I grabbed the rocket and twirled it around with my thumb and forefinger.

"But don't draw on it too strong," Caldonia warned me. "Don't want you going all funny-toed."

I toked on the rocket hard. My throat felt

like a hoover that had sucked up some hardcore sandpaper. I coughed and spluttered and coughed again. All of a sudden, my brain felt heavy. "Someone gimme water," I said.

Terror giggled out his ribs. Caldonia passed me her bottle of water. I almost emptied it.

"Liberties!" Caldonia complained. "You can buy me another one!"

I shook my head as we started again for Crongton Broadway.

We hit Blowhawk Lane ten minutes later. All of us had our baseball caps on – I could feel the darts of rain bouncing off mine. My heartbeat was pumping like a techno-dance tune. It felt like my Adam's apple was the size of a watermelon.

"Everyone good?" Terror asked.

"Of course," I lied.

Caldonia nodded.

We slowly rolled up Blowhawk Lane. The

breeze disturbed the litter on the street. The traffic huffed and puffed on the Broadway. Lovindeer's Lounge Bar received a liquor delivery. I glanced across the Broadway to the bank and recognised a vehicle pulling up further down. It had a bread and Jamaican patty symbol on its side. It was Mr Cassidy's van – Mum's boss. Mr Panic danced around in my head.

The hazard lights of Mr Cassidy's van blinked yellow. He climbed out of it and opened his umbrella. Mum got out of the passenger seat and walked around the front of the van to join Mr Cassidy. They linked arms. They smiled at each other.

He kissed her on the cheek.

She kissed him back. They full-stopped for a moment and gazed into each other's eyes.

I stopped dead in my trainers. It wasn't the rocket that had changed my legs to jelly. My eyes had a convo with my brain but my brain didn't wanna hear what my eyes had to say. Mr Panic was now booting the insides of my head.

"What is it?" Terror asked.

"My mum," I replied, nodding ahead.

Terror and Caldonia peered into the rain. Mr Cassidy and Mum entered the bank.

"They didn't see us, Briggy," Terror said. "If they did, they woulda hollered you out."

I tried to control my breathing but my heartbeat was doing a Bruce Lee *Enter the Dragon* thing.

"She ... she kissed him," I managed to say. "On the lips."

"I know it's traumatic," Caldonia said, "but can we save your *EastEnders* moment for later? We gotta step it up, Briggs."

"I feel for you," Terror said. "But I'm *not* aborting the mission."

I could feel Caldonia's hot glare as I stood, frozen. "Briggs!" Caldonia said. "We gotta move. We don't want too many peeps to see us stepping inside the post office, remember?"

I relived the kiss for three seconds before rolling on. I tried to dump it in a corner of my mind where things didn't really happen.

We made a left towards the post office. I glanced back to check that Mum and Mr Cassidy were still inside the bank, but a 159 bus covered the entrance.

Caldonia led the way. We reached the four steps that led to the post office. Terror closed the umbrella. He secured the button on it carefully. We stepped inside.

Wet footprints covered the floor. Four people were in the queue for the three counters that were open – including the euro one. An old woman with red gloves was posting about ten letters into the mailbox. A kid in a green anorak played with a spinner toy. The same staff as yesterday worked behind the counters – two women and the bald guy. We joined the line and Terror unzipped his bag a few centimetres. I did the same. Caldonia stood close behind us. My heartbeat vibrated my tonsils. Freezer-cold sweat formed on my back.

One woman had finished her business at counter number one. Three in the queue. And then us.

We shuffled up a bit. The floor was grimy. Three minutes later, there were two in the line before us. Terror flexed his fingers. I wiped my forehead. Caldonia pulled her cap down to shield her eyes.

A minute later, just one greyback lady was in front of us. She had a huge parcel to deliver. She had trouble carrying it. I could hear myself breathing. The wait for a counter to become free was as long as a double Chemistry class. I shifted from foot to foot. I realised that we hadn't planned what to say for this part of the mission. It wasn't even a sure thing that we'd get to roll up to the euro counter. I kept glancing at the entrance. Maybe Mum would stroll in arm-in-arm with Mr Cassidy any second. I hoped they did. I wouldn't have cared too much if she kissed him again, not if she could get my long ass outta this drama.

There was a clock on the wall: 9.32 a.m.

Counter two became free – the euro one was still busy. Terror was the first to move. I followed him. Caldonia was behind me. I guessed the woman behind the counter was in her thirties. Reddish-brown hair. She seemed to be wearing fake tan. Tired bags underlined her eyes. Her thin lips were cracked. She didn't look like she loved her job. She finished filling in a form and then looked up at Terror. My heart nearly came out of my chest and blitzed the counter glass.

"How can I help you?" the counter woman asked. She had a foreign accent. I couldn't guess where from. A name tag was pinned to her sky-blue shirt: *Gilda Smolenko*.

Terror pulled his gun from his bag and pointed it at Ms Smolenko. I did the same but I aimed it above her head. It was kinda dumb, cos I knew my gun was fake.

"Take out all the Gs from the till," Terror demanded in a low voice. "And pass them under the counter. *Don't* be slow."

Ms Smolenko squinted at the guns. Terror couldn't keep his weapon still. Then, I saw it. Terror's gun. Mr Panic was now biting my nerves and kicking my balls.

Terror's laser blaster had a dried blob of blackey-grey paint in the end of the barrel.

Ms Smolenko switched her glare to Terror and me. My eyelashes turned to hot ash.

"Do it *now*," Terror raised his voice.

"You *heard* him," Caldonia added. *"Now!"*

Ms Smolenko shook her head. "I *really* don't friggin need this today," she said. "Are you trying a funny one?"

Terror looked at me but I still couldn't find my tongue. Ms Smolenko stood up and pointed at Terror's gun. "That's about as real as my love life," she said. "I don't need this shit. You caught me on the wrong effing day!"

Terror and I swapped another glance. My brain begged me to run but my legs wanted to hear what Ms Smolenko had to say.

"Do you know what sort of week I've had?" Ms Smolenko carried on. "Yesterday, I had to pick up my boy from the police station cos he was caught selling pills at Johnny Osbourne's internet cafe. Not the first time I've had to take time off work to get my kid out of shit. And then my useless other half lost his job at the supermarket for nicking a tray of chicken thighs. Fat use his wages were anyway! I'm in debt to my ear-holes and now I'm being held up by a toy gun. *So you know what you can do? You can take your plastic toys and get the effing hell out of here!*"

Terror was the first to crack. He looked between Ms Smolenko and the exit, and then he bolted. A second later, Caldonia followed.

But I didn't move. I couldn't get my legs in motion.

Ms Smolenko sat back down on her stool and shook her head. "Effing teenagers!" she said.

Terror glanced back and screamed at me. "Briggy, *run!*"

At last my legs worked. I turned and hot-toed it to the door. But a crusty bruv, twice the size

of Terror, entered the post office just then. He
was wearing a blue helmet and a yellow Day-glo
jacket. His huge boots could have walked on top
of a giant beanstalk. Terror crashed into him,
lost his balance, slipped on the wet floor and
smacked his head on the wall. Then he fell to the
floor and lay there all zonked out.

Caldonia foot-slapped it outta there without
looking back, but I had to stop.

I knelt beside Terror and tried to raise him
up. He looked like he had taken ten more licks
from Caldonia's rocket – confused, vacant.

"Terror! Terror! Can you hear me?" I asked.

"Urrrgghhh," was all he replied.

I couldn't leave him.

I'm not sure how long I sat with Terror.
People crowded around me. Some of them were
cursing. Terror squinted at the light.

"Hooligans!" someone said.

"I dunno what's a matter with the kids today!" another added.

"They don't respect anything!"

"They tried to rob the post office!"

"Lock 'em all up!"

I don't know why, but Caldonia returned. I could see her there, slouching in the doorway, her dark eyes watching us.

"Someone get on the blower and call the police!" an angry voice yelled.

Caldonia and I swapped a glance. Somehow I knew she'd stay.

The next moment, we were all in a fed van being hot-wheeled to the station. Nobody spilled a word. Terror scoped the feds all around us. The bruise on the side of his face was turning blue.

"My mum's gonna murk me for this," Terror said.

I thought about what my mum, dad and Kingsley might do to my long ass. It wasn't pretty. A big part of my brain wanted the feds to keep me on lockdown for ever – so I never had to land my toes on home tiles again.

We pulled up at the back of the station. The tall wooden gates opened. We drove in. I was thinking about asking the feds to take Terror to hospital so he could be checked out. They didn't know he'd been sparked out for some long seconds. But I didn't ask. Fear had locked my tongue.

They took our fingerprints. Reality licked me hard. What had I been thinking?

I overheard a sergeant saying that they couldn't take us down to the cells cos we looked too young. They led us to a room and told us to sit down on a bench. They asked us for our names, ages and addresses. Terror and I did as we were told and I imagined Mum getting the call. I prayed she would take a time-out and simmer down before landing her vexed toes at the fed station.

Caldonia refused to leak any details. She gazed at the floor. Tears dripped down her cheeks. She kept on shaking her head.

"Just tell 'em," Terror said to Caldonia. "We're juveniles. They can't lock us down in Drumfort. The worse they can do is send us to juvenile detention."

Juvenile detention? I don't want to be wheeled away to any juvenile detention.

A female fed spoke softly to Caldonia. "The sooner you give us your name and address, the sooner this'll be over with. Come on, love. What's your name?"

Caldonia looked up. She wiped her face. "Caldonia Lake," she said in a whisper, "13 Sycamore Leaf Gardens, QE2 3SW."

That wasn't in South Crongton ends. Was she faking?

"We'll contact your parents right away," the fed said. "You won't be interviewed until they arrive. Can I get you a tea or something?"

"I'll have a Coke," Terror replied.

The fed shook her head and said, "I can get you a cup of water."

"That'll work." Terror nodded.

"I'll have the same," I said.

"And Caldonia?" the fed asked.

Caldonia went back to staring at the floor and mumbled, "Nothing for me."

Terror and me sipped our water. The female fed parked next to Caldonia. Two male blue bloods stood beside the door swapping whispers.

Half an hour later, the door opened. The sergeant we'd seen earlier walked in, along with a man dressed in a dark-blue suit. A blue tie gripped his neck and he had a blue handkerchief in his breast pocket. His shoes were shiny. He had a proper tan or he came from foreign ends – I couldn't tell. I sniffed, and the whiff of money filled my nostrils. "Caldonia," he called.

Caldonia looked up. She didn't look sad any longer – she looked angry. "You managed to pull yourself away from your bitch, then," Caldonia snapped. "Where's Mum?"

"She'll ... she'll be here when she can," the man replied.

Terror and I swapped a look. *Strange*.

"Why are you here?" Caldonia barked at the man. "*Don't* even pretend that you care."

"Your mother couldn't come right away, so she suggested that I get here now," the man said. "A parent has to be present while you're being questioned."

"You're not any freaking parent!" Caldonia yelled. "You walked out on us."

So this was Caldonia's Dad – Mr Lake.

"What's been going on here, Caldonia?" Mr Lake raised his voice. "There's no pleasing you, is there? You said you wanted to go to a state school. So we let you leave Joan Benson's and start at South Crongton. And this is what happens? You try to hold up a *post office?* Do you realise how much trouble you're in? Money can't sort this one out."

Caldonia narrowed her eyes. I sensed that she was loading her tongue. I was right – she delivered the cuss attack slow and steady. "Why don't you take all your pissing money and stick it up your secretary's business. Get outta my eyesight!"

Mr Lake looked at his shiny shoes. Caldonia folded her arms and turned to the wall.

"The sooner we get the interview done with, the sooner you'll be home," the sergeant said.

The female fed put a hand on Caldonia's arm and said, "Come on, love."

Two minutes later, Caldonia stood up. She looked at Terror for a long second. "It's not what you think," Caldonia began, "so don't scope me in that tone of voice. I wasn't playing the grime queen for jokes. I grew up in South East Crongton, had a hard-kerb life. But in the last few years, I'm not gonna lie, we've had money. One of Dad's business ideas worked for once. Trust me on this one – being rich is much better than being piss poor. I just wanted to help you get a sample of it. That's all. Sorry it led to this."

Terror looked like he didn't know how to respond. He just nodded.

"I don't think you'll see me after this," Caldonia said. "Dad will probably move me to some first-class ends and another stoosh school."

"I'm not sure if that'll be up to me," Mr Lake said to Caldonia. "The courts will have their say. Whatever's got into your head, I don't know."

Then they were gone.

I turned to Terror. Even after Caldonia's ghetto-queen confession, his eyes still had that glazed, love-bug look. "This is *her* fault, you know," I said to Terror. "*She* shouted us on all the way. Don't you remember what she said that day in detention?"

"Yeah, I remember," Terror said.

"She said *you two aren't shit-hot at anything*," I recalled. "She said that. Aren't you mad with her?"

Terror shook his head again and showcased his molars. Then he broke out into a mad chuckle. "I can never get the fury with Caldonia Lake," he said.

"Why?" I asked. "If it wasn't for her, this crazy mission would've never crashed into your head."

"Why?" Terror repeated. "I tell you why. You know my hard-kerb tale, Briggy. You know about all my fam's issues. My life was nothing. Going nowhere. Boring as a Sunday afternoon when the Wi-Fi doesn't work. My life started for real the first time Caldonia curled tongues with me. Now I think it's ending, cos I dunno if I'll bless my eyes on her ever again."

I didn't know what to say after that.

But I had to admit that I kinda let myself go along with the mission to get ratings from Caldonia Lake too.

Terror wasn't wrong. Caldonia Lake had made me feel alive, and she didn't even have to sample my lips.

CHAPTER ELEVEN

The Crongton Playhouse

Eight Months Later

It was the first time I had ever been to the
Crongton Playhouse.

I couldn't lie. Terror was a top-ranking actor.
His *Bugsy Malone* had a hard-kerb vibe to it. He
looked proper grown up in his three-piece suit,
hat and shiny shoes. Peeps in the place stood up
and clapped their palms off.

We agreed to link in the theatre cafe after his
performance.

He was half an hour late but I allowed him
that cos this brown-eyed chick wouldn't leave him

alone. I watched the actors mingle as I sipped my energy drink.

"Briggy!" Terror called when he spotted me. He had dressed back into his kerb-rat garms.

"Terror!" I replied.

He parked opposite me. We crashed fists. The brown-eyed chick didn't look too happy.

"It's been a while," Terror said. "A bredren told me the other day you've been landing on different ends."

"They weren't wrong," I replied. "Been travelling all over."

"Playing table tennis?" Terror guessed.

"Yep," I said. "Representing Biggin Spires."

"Isn't that a posho town?" Terror asked. "How did you get to represent them?"

Terror grabbed my bottle and tipped half of it down his throat. He hadn't changed.

"My dad lives in Biggin Spires now," I said.

"He's got a nine to five in the leisure centre there. He shares a place with my uncle. I visit Dad at weekends and I joined the table tennis club where he works."

"So things worked out for you," Terror said. "Luck kissed your ass when you found that table tennis table at youth detention."

"You're not wrong there," I said. "Luck blessed your behind too with those acting workshops you went to in detention. Those six months were worth it."

"Yeah, they were," Terror replied. "What about your situation at home? You know, with Cassidy?"

I didn't want Terror to go there.

"Come on, Briggy," Terror said. "What's the scene there?"

"Cassidy's always at home," I said. "He's trying to get on point with me but I can't get used to having him around. It's awkward to the max. It's a good thing I'm not there at weekends."

Terror shrugged. "That's how life goes, bruv. Welcome to the mash-up family zone! It's standard for Crongton."

I spotted the brown-eyed chick at the food counter. "So that's your new queen?" I asked.

Terror shook his head. "Nah. She'd like to be but you know my standards are high. How about you? Are you anywhere near the in-zone with Jennifer Caltrao yet?"

I couldn't kill my grin. "I'm getting there," I said. "I watched one of her netball games and she came to one of my table tennis matches. I asked her to come tonight but she's training."

"You're too slow, Briggy!" Terror said. "How long have we been out of the detention centre?"

"Two months," I replied.

"You need to get on the crash-mat with that

Jennifer or somebody else is gonna share that cheesecake in a six-star hotel with her."

"Not gonna happen," I said.

I wanted to change the subject. "Have you heard anything about Caldonia?" I asked.

Terror shook his head. The love bug was still there in his eyes. "No," he said. "Haven't heard a whisper or seen any chocolate lipstick. She's disappeared off the planet, bruv."

Terror fell silent. I felt sorry for him.

"Caldonia changed our lives for the better," Terror said. "Yep, the post office mission was cadazy, but look at us now. I'm stomping the boards and you're flapping at table tennis balls. One day you might get to meet Ma Long."

I nodded. "That would be neat," I said.

"I could hate the tiles Caldonia steps on," Terror said. "She did leave me hanging. But you know what, I don't."

"I don't hate her either," I said. "We're making our dent in this world. We *are* shit-hot at something."

"Wherever she is," said Terror. "I hope she's in a good place."

"Yeah, let me second that emotion," I said.

"And wherever she is," Terror said. "I bet on the acting awards I'm gonna get that she'll never take no crap from anyone."

"I agree with you on that one," I replied.

Terror closed his eyes as if he was remembering something. He opened them again.

"What a chick," he said.

"Yeah, what a chick," I repeated.

Our books are tested
for children and young people by
children and young people.

Thanks to everyone who consulted on
a manuscript for their time and effort in
helping us to make our books better
for our readers.